MUHAMMAD ALI

★ ★ ★ ★ ★ ★ ★ ★ ★

A CHAMPION IS BORN

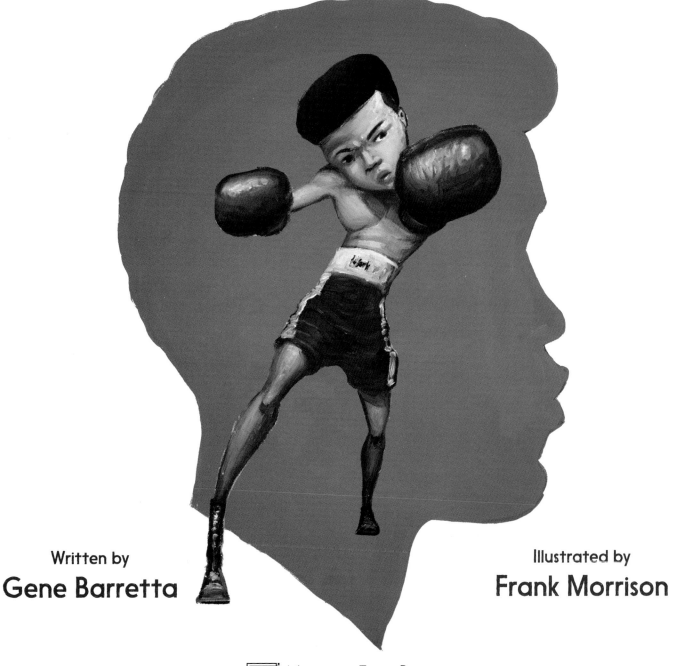

Written by
Gene Barretta

Illustrated by
Frank Morrison

KATHERINE TEGEN BOOKS
An Imprint of HarperCollins Publishers

For my personal champion, Benjamin Adam Barretta.
Love, Dad.
—G.B.

To my children, my champs: Nia, Tiffani, Nyree, Tyreek, and Nasir.
Be good! Be great!

—F.M.

HarperCollins
PUBLISHERS
Since 1817

Photograph credits: page 38: AP Images; 39: AP Images/REX/Shutterstock

Katherine Tegen Books is an imprint of HarperCollins Publishers.

Muhammad Ali: A Champion Is Born
Text copyright © 2017 by Gene Barretta
Illustrations copyright © 2017 by Frank Morrison

Library of Congress Control Number: 2016949686
ISBN 978-0-06-243016-8

The artist used oil on illustration board to create the illustrations for this book.   Typography by Rachel Zegar
16 17 18 19 20 PC/PC 10 9 8 7 6 5 4 3 2 1 ❖ First Edition

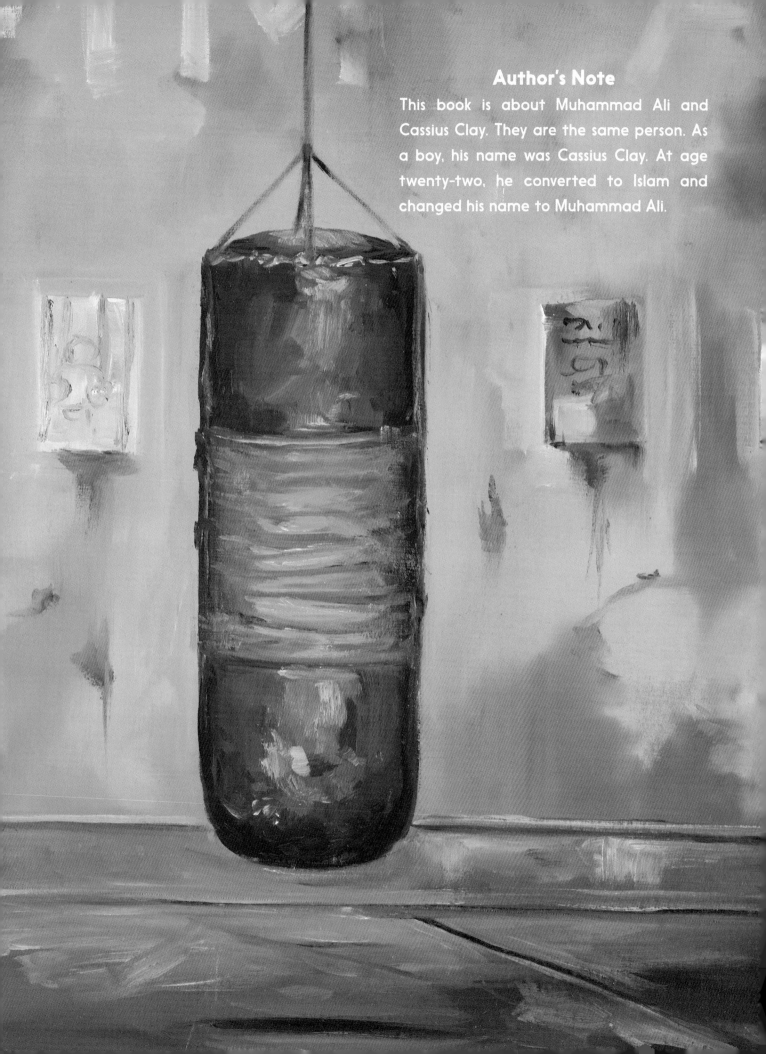

Author's Note
This book is about Muhammad Ali and Cassius Clay. They are the same person. As a boy, his name was Cassius Clay. At age twenty-two, he converted to Islam and changed his name to Muhammad Ali.

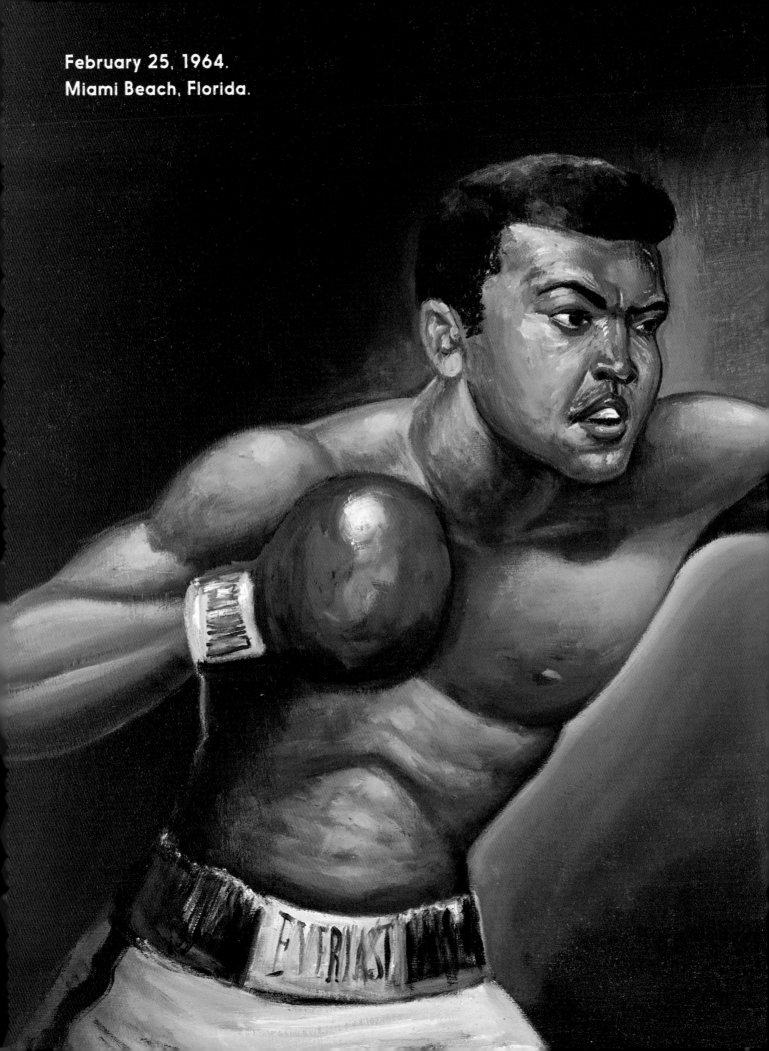

February 25, 1964.
Miami Beach, Florida.

POW!

CASSIUS CLAY bounces around the ring on the balls of his feet, throwing jabs and dodging uppercuts from champion Sonny Liston. Clay is the clear underdog. But after six intense rounds, he surprises everyone and wins the world heavyweight championship.

"I SHOOK UP THE WORLD!"

May 25, 1965.
Lewiston, Maine.

POW! POW!

The two boxers meet for a rematch. Only, Clay has a new name—the name of a champion—Muhammad Ali. It means "worthy of praise—most high." Ali wins again.

"I AM THE GREATEST!"

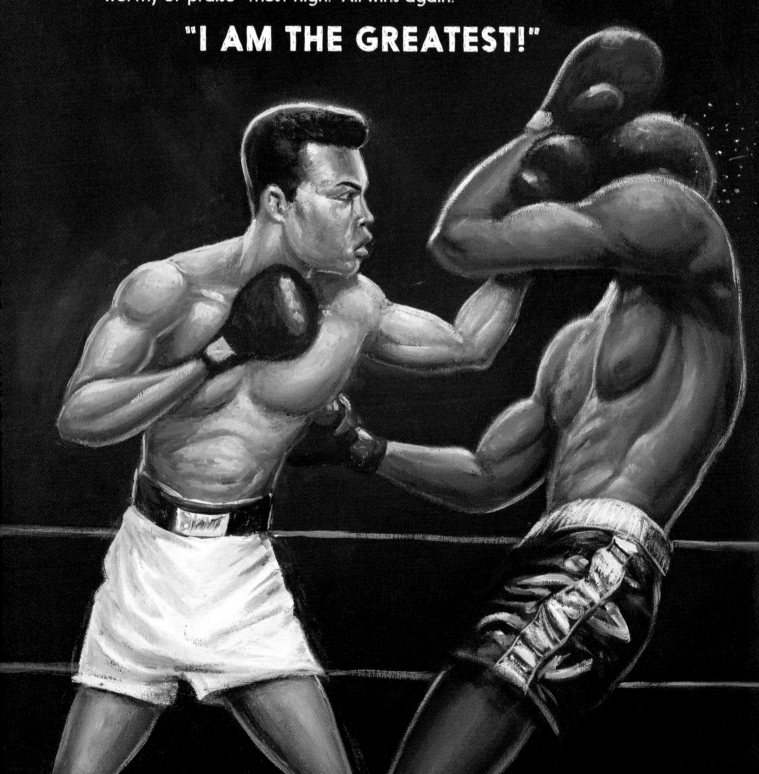

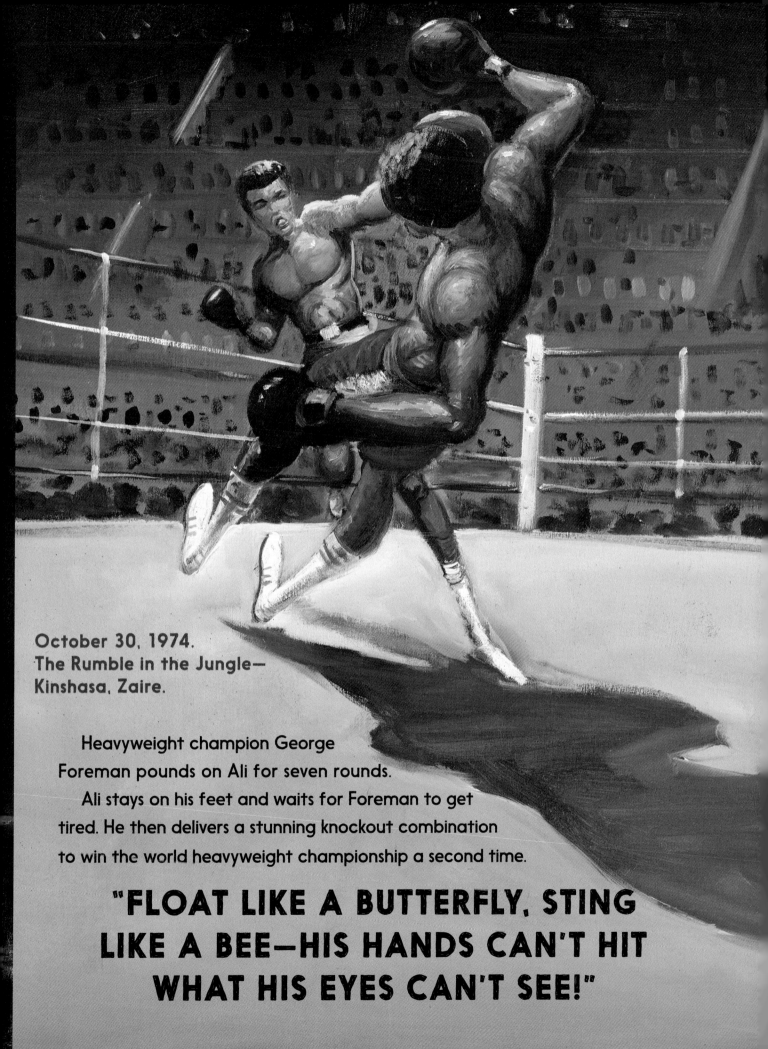

October 30, 1974.
The Rumble in the Jungle—
Kinshasa, Zaire.

Heavyweight champion George
Foreman pounds on Ali for seven rounds.
Ali stays on his feet and waits for Foreman to get
tired. He then delivers a stunning knockout combination
to win the world heavyweight championship a second time.

"FLOAT LIKE A BUTTERFLY, STING LIKE A BEE—HIS HANDS CAN'T HIT WHAT HIS EYES CAN'T SEE!"

September 15, 1978.
New Orleans, Louisiana.

POW!
POW!
POW!

At age thirty-six, near the end of his career, Ali wins a rematch against champion Leon Spinks to become the first boxer to win the world heavyweight championship three times.

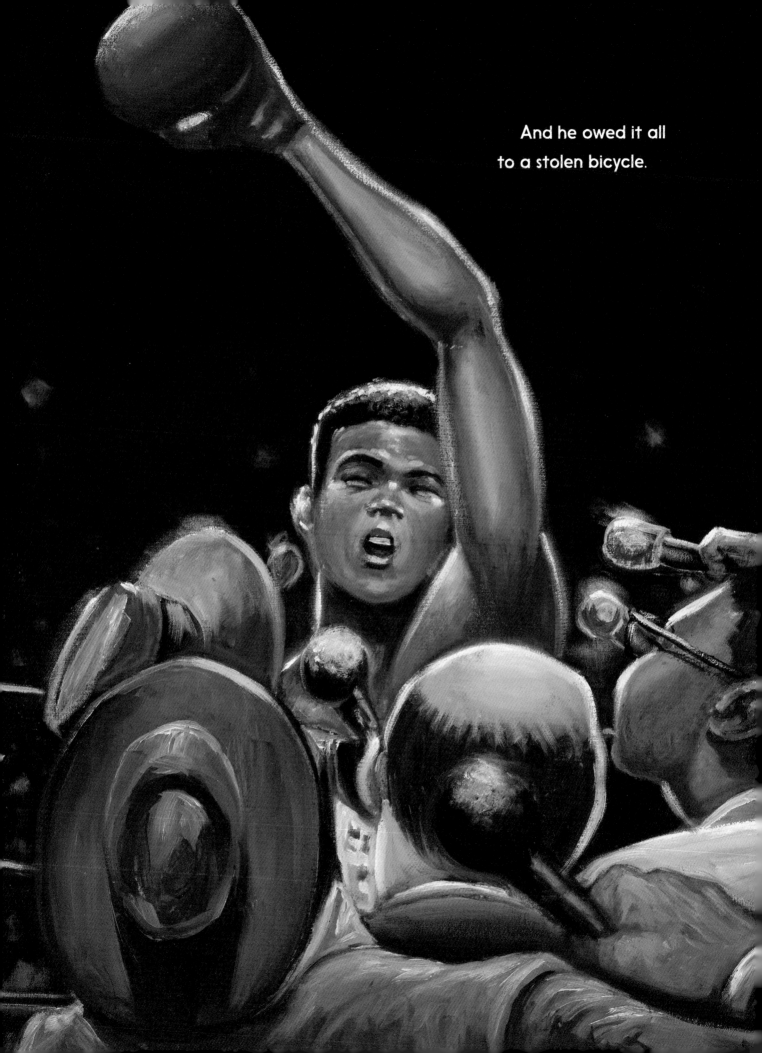

And he owed it all
to a stolen bicycle.

Winter 1954.
Home of twelve-year-old Cassius Clay—
Louisville, Kentucky.

"Hurry up! Before they eat all the popcorn!"
Cassius yelled as he raced to the Louisville Home
Show on his brand-new bike.

"And the hot dogs too! Wait up!" answered his best
friend, Johnny.

"Don't worry, I'll save you the bun," Cassius joked.

A heavy rain soaked the streets, but nothing slowed
them down.

Cassius felt cool on his bike. The new chrome shined brighter when it was wet.
He rolled up to the home show and hit his brakes hard. The front tire kicked up a wave of water.

He looked back at Johnny.

"Did you really think you could beat me? Not only can I ride fast, but I look good doin' it."

They hopped off their bikes and ran inside.

The Louisville Home Show was an annual bazaar. It was held for all the black merchants, who were not allowed to attend or sell their products at the white bazaars.

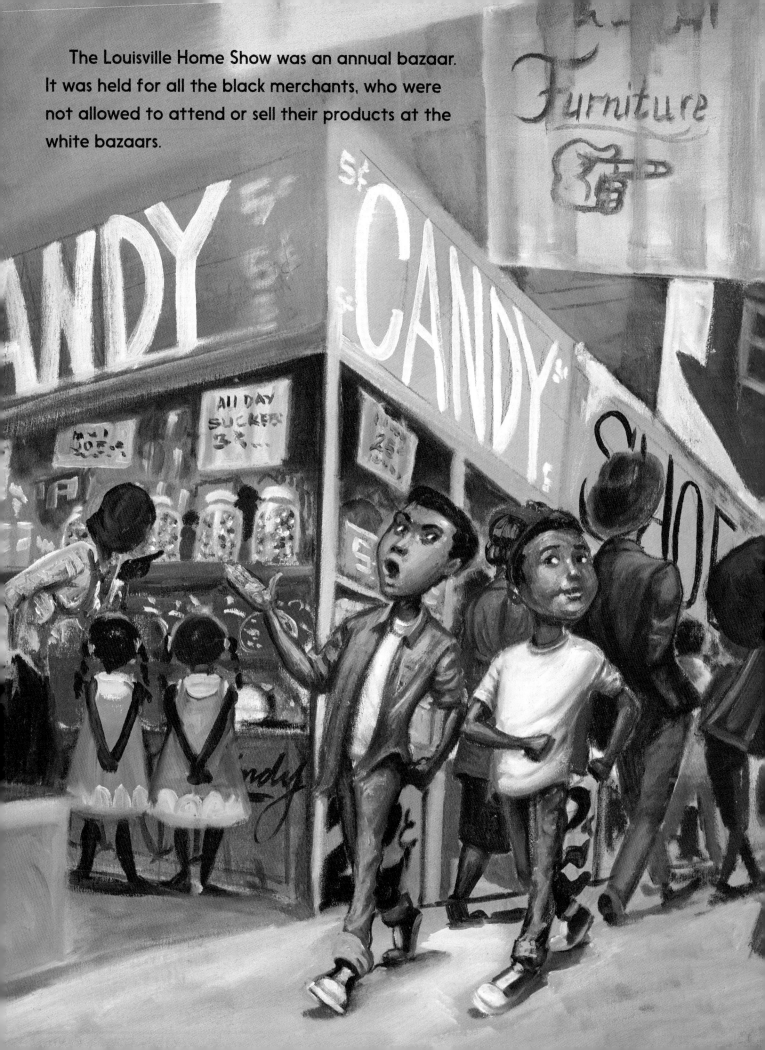

Segregation was as real as the rain in Louisville, and Cassius saw how his people suffered for it. He spoke proudly of them. "I know why they won't let us in the white bazaars. Because they're afraid we'll show them up."

He pointed to every booth and said, "One day I'm gonna get one of those and one of those and one of those.

"But right now, I have room for one more free hot dog before . . . Oh no! Dinner! We're late. We gotta get home."

They stepped outside and Cassius froze in his tracks. "No!" he shouted as he looked in every direction. "My bike! Where's my bike?"

Cassius ran up the street. "Did you see a red bike? Did you see anyone with my new red bike?" His eyes welled up with tears. "I need a policeman!"

Finally, an older woman spoke up. "Go back in the building and go down to the basement. Ask for Officer Joe Martin."

He found Officer Martin and explained every last detail. "It was red and white, with whitewall tires and chrome. . . . I just got it for Christmas and there wasn't a mark on it." His fists were clenched tight like hammers. He raised his voice. "And when I find whoever took my bike, I'm gonna whup him!"

Cassius was small and thin. Officer Martin looked him over and offered some advice. "Listen, son. Before you whup somebody, you better learn to fight."

That was not what Cassius expected to hear, especially from a police officer.

It took a moment for him to catch his
breath and look around. Then it all made sense.
For the very first time, Cassius Clay was standing
inside a boxing gym.

The energy in the room made his heart race. He loved
the sound of boxing gloves smacking the speed bag and the
rhythm of the jump ropes slapping the floor. He loved the shuffling
feet of the shadowboxers and the smell of rubbing alcohol in the air.

DING! DING!

A bell rang and two young guys started bobbin' and weavin' in the ring. *Wow*, thought Cassius.

Photos of old boxing champions stared out at Cassius, as if to say, "Let's go a few rounds."

"We're here every weeknight if you want to join us," Martin said.

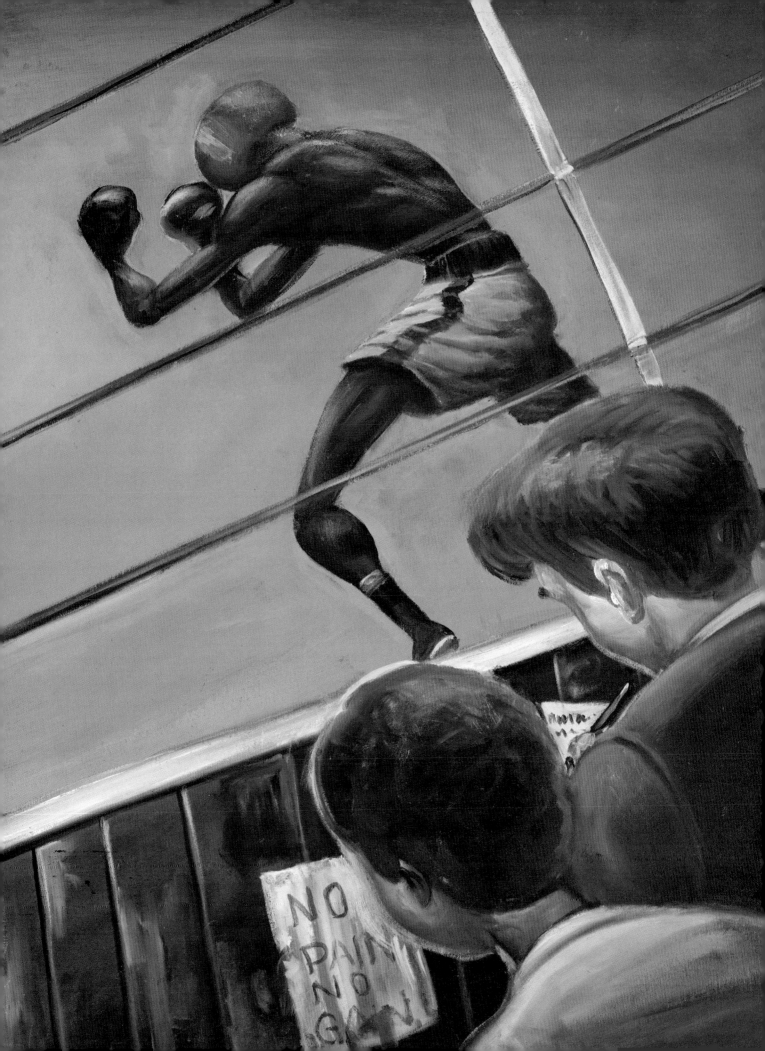

On the way home, Johnny kept repeating, "You're gonna get it when you get home. Boy, you're gonna get it."

And he did. His dad pitched a fit so loud it echoed off the neighbor's house. Cassius heard every word, but his mind was really on the boxing gym.

A few days later, he was shocked to see the same gym on a local TV show called *Tomorrow's Champions.*

"Look!" he said to his mother. "That's the gym. That's Officer Martin. He trains the boys."

Cassius got so excited he threw on his jacket and dashed out the door. "I want to be a boxer!"

As he leaped across the old porch, Cassius called out to his mom, "I'm gonna win big and buy you a brand-new porch at the home show. No, wait. I'm gonna buy you a brand-new home at the home show!"

His brother, Rudy, went racing after him. "Wait for me!"

From that point on, all Cassius thought about was boxing. He told all the kids at school, "You're looking at the next world champion."

They just laughed at him and joked, "Uh-oh! Somebody must have punched him too hard. He thinks he's Sugar Ray Robinson."

"Wait, Cassius, did you say *champ* or *chump*?" they teased.

"Ha ha ha!"

Cassius imagined his name being broadcast from the intercom. "*Ladies and gentlemen, Cassius Clay! Heavyweight champion of the world!*"

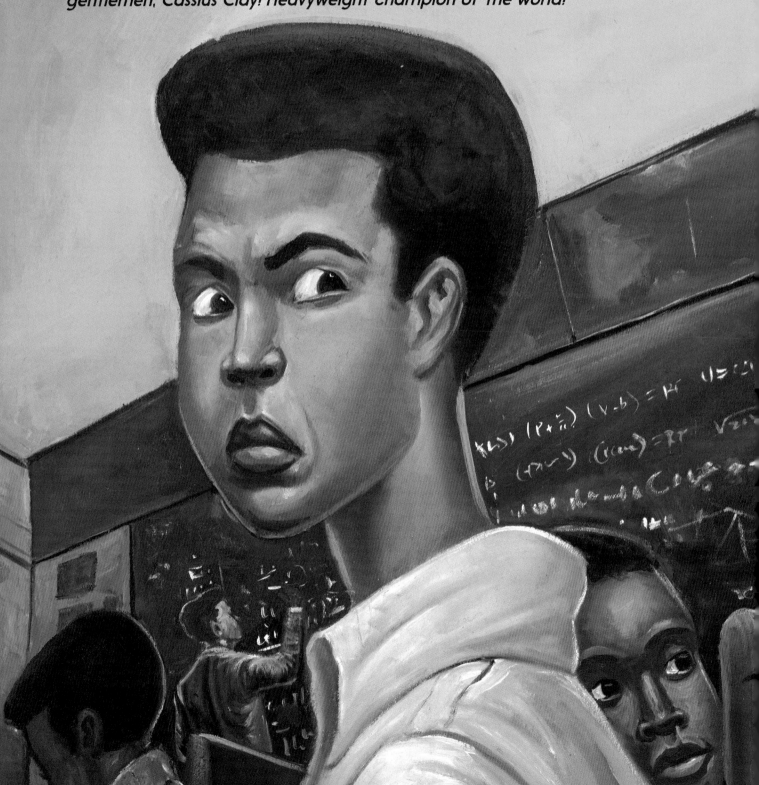

He drew pictures of boxing robes with the words *Cassius Clay, Heavyweight Champion of the World* on the back. He knew that one day he would wear that robe.

Cassius worked hard with Officer Martin every day after school. He hit the speed bag, jumped rope, and practiced shadowboxing. "Watch this. I can move faster than my own shadow."

Cassius had his own style of training at home. On most mornings, his workout started before sunrise. He often ran alongside the school bus to build up his endurance.

Sometimes Rudy would throw stones at Cassius to test his reflexes. "Come on, Rudy! I'm not the invisible man. Why can't you hit me?"

Every night after Martin's gym closed up, Cassius headed to a second trainer, named Fred Stoner. Cassius told Rudy, "Fred Stoner's boys are winning all the fights in Louisville."

With Stoner, he improved his jabs, uppercuts, and hooks. He learned the cross, the bolo, the clinch, bobbing, weaving, and the peek-a-boo.

Training was hard. But Cassius said to himself,

"DON'T QUIT. SUFFER NOW AND LIVE THE REST OF YOUR LIFE AS A CHAMPION."

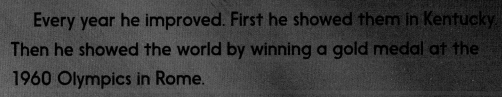

Every year he improved. First he showed them in Kentucky.
Then he showed the world by winning a gold medal at the
1960 Olympics in Rome.

That was only the beginning. During his legendary boxing
career, he won fifty-six out of sixty-one professional fights.

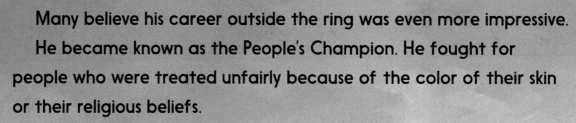

Many believe his career outside the ring was even more impressive. He became known as the People's Champion. He fought for people who were treated unfairly because of the color of their skin or their religious beliefs.

He wanted to be a positive role model for them.

"I HAD TO PROVE YOU COULD BE A NEW KIND OF BLACK MAN. I HAD TO SHOW THE WORLD."

His words of peace, pride, and human decency inspired people from all over the world.

They called him Champ, and it felt great.

It felt as great as racing down a Louisville street on a brand-new red-and-white bicycle with whitewall tires and shiny chrome trim.

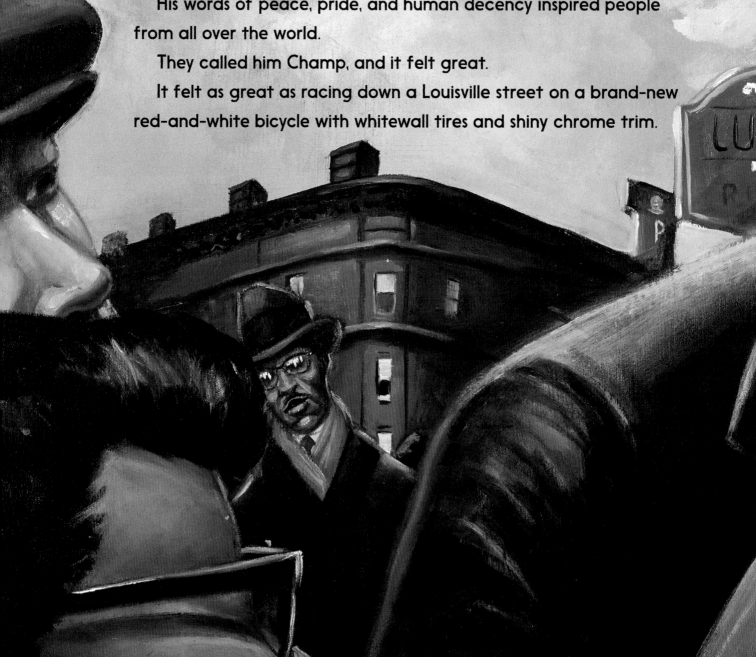

Cassius Clay, 1954

A powerful force both in and out of the ring, Muhammad Ali was one of the most important athletes of the twentieth century.

His boxing style was as unique as his personality.

IN THE RING, Ali bounced swiftly on his toes, just like when he was a boy.

The Champ was born Cassius Marcellus Clay Jr. on January 17, 1942, in Louisville, Kentucky. They called him GG, because that was the sound he made as a baby.

His father, Cassius Sr., and mother, Odessa, made a loving home for their son and his brother, Rudy. Still, it was impossible to shield them from the racial segregation that existed in Louisville and the rest of the country. At an early age, Cassius learned firsthand the definition of injustice. Yet in the face of extreme prejudice, the boys were raised to feel a great deal of pride and self-awareness.

Cassius brought that confidence into the ring. He joked that GG really stood for Golden Gloves. As an amateur boxer, he won several Golden Gloves and Amateur Athletic Union titles. As a pro, Ali won three heavyweight championships, which he defended nineteen times.

During a period when fighters let their managers speak for them, Ali spoke freely. His provocative and entertaining style earned him the nickname the Louisville Lip. He would often predict the outcome of his fights with rhymes. Ali taunted champion Sonny Liston, "He might be great, but he'll fall in eight."

His fights were worldwide events, as popular as the Super Bowl today. Some of them were promoted with catchy names, like the "Fight of the Century" against Joe Frazier in 1971, the "Rumble in the Jungle" against George Foreman in 1974, and the "Thrilla in Manila" against Frazier again in 1975.

During the 1960s and 1970s, he was the most recognizable athlete on the globe.

IN THE RING, Ali circled his opponent with his gloves down, as if to say, "I've got nothing to hide; bring it on." That was also how he lived his life. He had the courage to speak his mind on matters of race and religion during the turbulent civil rights movement of the 1960s.

Although Cassius Clay was raised a Baptist, he developed a spiritual connection with Islam in the 1960s and became a Muslim. As part of his devotion, he changed his name to Muhammad Ali in 1964. Initially, he joined the Nation of Islam, a religious movement that spoke out boldly against discrimination and racism. Ali faced much criticism for his views and was willing to put his boxing career in jeopardy to defend them.

In 1967, Ali was drafted to become a soldier in the Vietnam War but refused to go based on his religious beliefs. Consequently, he was convicted of a felony and went to court to avoid jail time. His championship title was taken away and his boxing license was suspended. For many years it was a struggle for him to make a living and pay expensive legal fees.

IN THE RING, Ali skillfully dodged his opponents' punches. He stood his ground and did not back away. Outside the ring, he also stood his ground and continued to fight for his civil and religious rights until the Supreme Court overturned his conviction.

In 1971, he was free to continue his boxing career. During that difficult period, his boxing fans remained loyal. Ali also gained new fans because of the way he promoted

Muhammad Ali, 1966

dignity and respect in underprivileged communities throughout the world.

After he retired from boxing in 1981, he continued to build his legacy as a humanitarian and social activist, both nationally and globally.

His Muslim faith remained a source of strength throughout his life, especially in 1984, when at the age of forty-two he was diagnosed with Parkinson's disease. Ali viewed his condition as a calling to become a positive role model for others facing the disease.

In 2005, the Muhammad Ali Center opened in his hometown of Louisville to feature exhibits about Ali's life and career, as well as to inspire people to be as great as they can be.

Muhammad Ali passed away on June 3, 2016. A week later, thousands of people said a final good-bye as his funeral procession passed through the streets of Louisville. Ali is survived by his wife, Lonnie, and nine children.

BIBLIOGRAPHY

Ali, Muhammad with Hana Yasmeen Ali. *The Soul of a Butterfly: Reflections of Life's Journey.* New York: Simon & Schuster, 2004.

Ali, Muhammad with Richard Durham. *The Greatest: My Own Story.* New York: Graymalkin Media, 2015.

Hauser, Thomas. *Muhammad Ali: His Life and Times.* New York: Simon & Schuster, 1991.

I Am Ali. Directed by Clare Lewins. Focus Features, 2014.

READ MORE ABOUT MUHAMMAD ALI

Books

Ali, Maryum "May May." Illustrated by Patrick Johnson. *I Shook Up the World: The Incredible Life of Muhammad Ali.* Hillsboro, OR: Beyond Words, 2003.

Myers, Walter Dean. *The Greatest: Muhammad Ali.* New York: Scholastic, 2001.

Smith, Jr., Charles R. Illustrated by Bryan Collier. *Twelve Rounds to Glory: The Story of Muhammad Ali.* Somerville, MA: Candlewick, 2007.

Websites

www.muhammadali.com

www.history.com/topics/black-history/muhammad-ali